Mr Barafund

and the

Rockdragon

Julie Rainsbury & Graham Howells

Pont

First Impression – 2005
Reprinted – 2008, 2015

ISBN 978 1 84323 449 4

This title is published with the financial support of the
Welsh Books Council.

Printed in Wales at
Gomer Press, Llandysul, Ceredigion SA44 4JL
www.gomer.co.uk

Mr Barafundle frowned. He opened both eyes and stretched his oh-so-round body in his oh-so-comfy bed. He frowned again. Mr Barafundle's face didn't fit easily into a frown. He was usually the most happy-as-the-day-is-long creature imaginable. He hardly ever, almost never, frowned. Something had disturbed him but, now he was awake, he couldn't quite put his thumb on it.

Mr Barafundle climbed out of bed and sang his good morning song to the sea.

He dressed in the fresh-pressed clothes he'd laid out the night before, then ruffled and rumpled his hair until it stood out around his face in jolly spikes – just the way he liked it. In the mirror, Mr Barafundle's beam changed back into a frown. A moan of sound flooded the room:

a wail, a so-sad-sob,

a hiccup, a sniff,

a great, grievous groan.

Mr Barafundle flung open the shutters. Outside, all was as it should be. The sun smiled, seagulls chuckled in the sky, the sea giggled against pebbles on the beach and Mr Barafundle's island home rocked in time to the tide and a new day's laughter. Then the eerie sound echoed once more across the bay:

a wail, a so-sad-sob, a hiccup, a sniff, a great, grievous groan.

Mr Barafundle ran outside and climbed up the tree ladders in the mighty oak to his look-out post. He took his telescope and turned in a slow circle, scanning horizons where sky met sea, where sea met land, where land met sky.

'There!' He let out a triumphant yell.

On a far headland, he spied a sharp blaze of red, a wraith of smoke.

'A distress signal!'

Mr Barafundle tuned his island in to the power of the great bluestones and floated off across the bay until he anchored safely under the headland.

The dreadful, despairing sound grew louder and louder as Mr Barafundle climbed towards the cliff-top:

a wail, a so-sad-sob, a hiccup, a sniff, a great, grievous groan.

Mr Barafundle stopped in surprise. He had expected to see fire on top of the cliff – a flickering, smoking beacon.

'A young rockdragon,' exclaimed Mr Barafundle. 'What are you doing here? You should have flown south for the winter long ago.'

The rockdragon backed away. He shook fearfully. He looked around but there was nowhere to hide. He wailed and sobbed. He hiccupped and sniffed. He moaned and groaned. Huge teardrops slid down his cheeks and plopped onto his taloned toes. He beat his baby wings. His scaly body flared and flamed crimson as he twisted this way and that, seeking an escape. His spiky tail drooped disconsolately. Between each wail and sob, each hiccup and sniff, each moan and groan, he sighed billows of smoke that drifted high above the cliff-top and out to sea, veiling all the sky's brightness like storm-cloud.

'What on earth's the matter?'

Mr Barafundle reached out and touched the rockdragon's shoulder oh-so-gently. The rockdragon shivered and shuddered and wailed even louder.

'Now, now!' shouted Mr Barafundle kindly. 'I'm sure things can't be as bad as all that. Do stop crying, there's a good rock-dragon, you're beginning to give me a headache.'

Mr Barafundle stroked the rockdragon's damp cheek. The rockdragon hiccupped and sniffed. His loud wailing quietened . . . a little.

'What's your name?' asked Mr Barafundle.

'H-haven't g-got one,' sobbed the rockdragon. 'I'm too young to have been given a proper name yet and now they've l-left me behind and I'll n-never have a name of m-my own. All my rockdragon family had names, all my rockdragon neighbours had names, all my rockdragon friends had names. And now I c-c-can't have one . . .'

The rockdragon's sobbing was in danger of becoming a wail again.

'But that's easily sorted,' said Mr Barafundle. 'Never say *can't* when *can* is possible. I can give you a name.'

'You can?'

The rockdragon's tearful eyes became round and shiny. He hiccupped. He sniffed. He stopped sobbing altogether. He shook his scales dry, flicked the last teardrops from the tips of his sixteen talons, clapped his wings and rubbed his sharp snout timidly along Mr Barafundle's arm.

'I've got a pocketful of names here somewhere,' said Mr Barafundle.

He drew out a handful of scraps of parchment, paper and glossy card.

'Catch one you fancy,' he said.

Mr Barafundle cupped the spangle of names in both hands. With a hop, skip and jump, he started to dance a jig around the rockdragon. In time to the beat of his big, brown boots, he spun each name into the air, one after another:

'Brynberian, Cilgerran, Marloes or Bosheston,
Nevern, Dinas, Rhoscrowther or Puncheston,
Milford, Mathry, Carn Ingli, or Bletherston,
Cemaes, Cilgwyn, Preseli or Clarbeston,
Govan, Solva, Maenclochog or Letterston,
Cleddau, Wiston, Stackpole or …'

'Stop! Stop!'

The rockdragon stared up at the scraps shifting on the breeze like a fall of rainbow snow. He reared up on his hind legs and stretched out his front claws as high as they would go. One talon-tip clipped the last scarlet scrap that Mr Barafundle had thrown and sent it drifting down towards the gorse. The rockdragon pounced.

'Stackpole!' he shouted. 'I want to be Stackpole!'

He bounded over to Mr Barafundle and gave him the scrap.

'Let's see then.'

Mr Barafundle fumbled in his waistcoat pocket and popped his reading glasses on the end of his nose. He smoothed the scarlet paper and peered at the name written on it.

'Stackpole it is!' he exclaimed. 'Stackpole the Rockdragon.'

He danced another jig around Stackpole, singing the rock-dragon's new name and beating out each syllable with his big, brown boots.

Then, above the sound of his singing and the beat of his boots, Mr Barafundle became aware of another noise:

a wail, a so-sad-sob,

a hiccup, a sniff,

a great, grievous groan.

Mr Barafundle stopped dancing.

'What's the matter now, Stackpole? I thought you wanted a name?'

'I d-did. I d-do,' wept Stackpole, 'b-but I'll still get called all the other names . . . Cry-maybe, Cowardly-mustard and Scaredy-bat . . . b-because I'll still be all those things. That's really why I had no proper name and that's why I've been left behind.

'Other rockdragons are given their names on the day they learn to fly, just before the great dragon-flock takes to the air and heads south for the winter. But I've never been able to fly and . . .' Stackpole's scales blushed to an even deeper crimson. He hung his head and continued in a shamed whisper, '. . . whoever heard of a rockdragon who can't fly?'

'I'm sure you'll manage it one day,' said Mr Barafundle. 'I mean, you're only a very small rockdragon at the moment.'

'And a cry-maybe, a cowardly-mustard, a scaredy-bat . . .' sobbed Stackpole. 'I can't do anything right.'

'Never say *can't* when *can* is possible,' said Mr Barafundle.

Stackpole stopped crying. His eyes grew round and shiny.

'Can you teach me to fly?' he asked. 'I'm sure I'd manage it if you told me what to do. Then I could soar away south and catch up with the dragon-flock and tell them my new name and they'd never be able to call me a good-for-nobody ever again.'

Mr Barafundle shook his head.

'I don't think I can teach you to fly, Stackpole. I don't know much about flying myself and . . .' he glanced at the rockdragon, '. . . your wings really do need to grow a bit.

'Now don't start all that wailing again. There must be something you're good at. There's no point spending all your time being miserable. What can you do that will cheer you up until the dragon-flock returns?'

'I c-can't do anything. I really am a good-for-nobody, a cry-maybe, a cowardly-mustard, a scare . . .'

Mr Barafundle grabbed Stackpole by his two front claws and danced another jig, spinning the rockdragon round and round with him. Stackpole gasped for breath and was so surprised that he stopped sobbing.

'I'm no good at flying,' laughed Mr Barafundle, 'but I am good at dancing, and dancing always makes me happy. I've never met a rockdragon yet who could dance for toffee – so I'm sure, if we practised, you could be the best rockdragon-dancer in the whole, wide world!'

'But I can't, I can't . . .' puffed Stackpole as he was jostled and jiggled around.

Mr Barafundle took no notice.

Mr Barafundle tapped a brown-booted toe,
Wiggled his hips, said: *Let yourself go!*
He held Stackpole tight by one spiky claw,
Told him to imagine they were on a dance floor.
He stepped to the left; he stepped to the right,
But Stackpole still trembled, quivered with fright.
Mr Barafundle demonstrated a turn
But the rockdragon sobbed it was too hard to learn.
Mr Barafundle called out: *Follow me!*
Counted aloud: *One, two, three. One, two, THREE!*
He clicked his fingers and clapped his hands
But Stackpole still claimed he could not understand.
A dance can sweep trouble clean from your mind,
Sang Mr Barafundle. But Stackpole plodded behind.
He moaned: *I've got wings, a tail and four feet,*
So my rockdragon dancing will never be great.

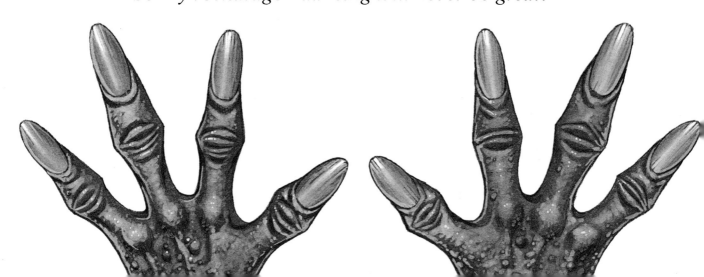

Mr Barafundle sighed and stopped dancing.

'You've got to try, Stackpole,' he said.

The rockdragon shuffled his four left feet helplessly. He tripped over his tail and sent it tangling amongst his wings like spaghetti.

'I am trying but it's hard and I just . . . CAN'T!'

Mr Barafundle watched as Stackpole huffed and puffed, wriggled and jiggled, pulling the knots in his legs, wings and tail tighter and tighter.

'Mmm . . . never say *can't* when *can* is possible,' he said, 'but sometimes . . . things take a little while and need . . . a smidgeon of help. Come on, follow me.'

Stackpole stood still, unravelled his body, shook out his scales, then trotted off behind Mr Barafundle.

They walked for a long time. They walked past bays, across meadows, up hills, down valleys, around hamlets, over rivers, through caves, beneath castles. They walked in sunshine and in shadow. They walked all day and all night. They walked along roads, lanes, bridleways, tracks and footpaths that seemed, to Stackpole, to roll out in front of them forever.

At last they came to a vast forest.

'It looks dark.'

Stackpole peered into the forest from behind Mr Barafundle's back.

'It looks dreadful.'

He started to shiver and shake and hiccupped a small sob.

'It looks so very . . . dangerous.'

'Of course it does,' said Mr Barafundle. 'It's magic – and magic can be dark and dreadful and dangerous. But it can be light too.

'It's true, I must admit, that the Gobblings love to lurk in this forest, but it's also full of goodness and fair folk. Then there are all the in-between creatures. There are the Coydwig, for instance, when you can find them. They're secretive and mischievous but they're also full of fun and laughter and never mean serious harm.

'And there's Hakin the witch, of course. She's the one we've come to see. She can be a powerful force for good – when she feels like it.'

Stackpole let out a wail, a so-sad-sob, a great, grievous groan.

'I don't want to go into the d-deep, deep darkness . . . and you don't seem very sure that this Hakin will help us. I d-don't think I want to meet a real, live w-w-witch.'

'Sh-sh,' Mr Barafundle hushed him. 'We'll be fine. The Gobblings like to sleep during the day. Still, *Better a Gobbling asleep than a Gobbling awake*, as the old saying goes – so I'd really rather you didn't disturb them.'

Mr Barafundle strode ahead. Stackpole gulped, he hiccupped, he sniffed. He sighed a small but dismal cloud of smoke. He didn't want to venture into the forest but he didn't want to be left behind on his own either. Slowly, and as silently as he could, he tip-toed after Mr Barafundle on his sixteen twitching talons.

Witch Hakin's house stood, coddled in mosses, lichen, leaf-mould, in the deepest dark of the forest. The way leading to its door was steep and stony, guarded by the unblinking eyes of owls.

Yet waterfalls, long and sleek as maiden-hair, plashed down to a silvered stream. Shafts of sunlight crowned the roof-straw gold and sparked all the windows into welcome.

'It's scary,' said Stackpole, 'but sort of . . . sort of beautiful too.'

'That's magic for you,' said Mr Barafundle. 'Hakin! Hakin! We need your help!'

Mr Barafundle rapped boldly on the iron-bound door, while Stackpole cowered among some nearby tree roots.

Hakin was in a good mood. Once she had invited them in and chided her staff-owl for pecking at Stackpole's tail, Hakin settled them down in front of the fire with steaming mugs of whinberry tea and an enormous slice of chestnut and wild mushroom pie. She listened carefully to Mr Barafundle as he told Stackpole's story and his plan to teach the rockdragon to dance.

'Rockdragons have never been known for their dancing,' said Hakin dubiously.

She walked around Stackpole and studied him from every angle while her staff-owl nipped at his knees.

'And this one will need all the help we can give him. He's such an extremely stocky, horribly sturdy little rockdragon, after all, with no daring or dash about him. He has none of the full-grown grace of the dragon-flock.'

Stackpole's scales burned with a bright blush of crimson. Every one of his sixteen talons curled in embarrassment.

'Please don't upset him,' said Mr Barafundle. 'It might make him wail again.'

'I'm not trying to upset him,' said Hakin huffily. 'I'm just telling-it-like-it-is.'

'But you know how wonderful it can be to dance,' said Mr Barafundle in a soft voice that was full of subtle music. 'How exciting and magical it is. You must remember how the two of us danced and danced until midnight and beyond all those years ago at the Snow-solstice Ball . . .'

Hakin shook her head and interrupted him briskly, but Stackpole noticed that she was smiling again.

'That was indeed many, many, many moons ago,' she said, 'when the trees of this forest were still saplings, when my hair was as bright as a fall of water in sunlight, when I needed no staff-owl to ease my aching limbs.'

Still, Mr Barafundle's words seemed to have persuaded Hakin to help. She hobbled over to the high shelves that lined the room and lifted down bottles of luminous syrups, jars of jewel-stained powders, mysterious caskets that rattled with darkness. A snuff of dust, of ash, sifted across the floor as she carried bundles of dried herbs to the hearth.

As Hakin worked, she hummed to herself, murmured the rhythmic sounds of a dancing spell. Her enormous cooking pot bubbled above the fire. From a crystal ewer, she poured streams of quicksilver, stirred in splashes of syrup, pinches of powder. She picked seven black stones, counted seven bleached bones, grasped handfuls of herbs. Slowly she drowned them all in a stew of magic that was thickened by her words, her music. At last the mixture was ready. Hakin lifted a ladle full of midnight: an indigo liquid, sticky, with a sheen of violet, the glint of myriad stars.

Hakin dipped the barb of Stackpole's tail into the ladle – painted each of his sixteen talons until they glowed, so long, so lustrous. Stackpole flexed his taloned fingers and twiddled his taloned toes. They twinkled with energy – like fairy lights. His scales flickered, shone, blazed neon. He itched and twitched with excitement until he just couldn't sit still for a moment longer.

Stackpole the rockdragon started to twist,
Spun Hakin about with a flick of his wrist.
He tapped out a tap dance across the flagged floor,
Rocked around the clock from eleven till four.
He leapt with a grace that was almost balletic,
Danced on his points, arabesqued, pirouetted.
He invited Witch Hakin to cha-cha, to waltz,
Twirled into a quick-step – leading, of course.
Mr Barafundle soon joined in the fun,
They all danced together, they danced one by one,
They linked for a conga and kicked up their heels
Line-dancing, folk-dancing, dancing wild reels.
They boogied, they discoed and tried out hip-hop,
They broke into break-dancing – unable to stop.

They danced in a circle, they danced in a square,
Charlestoned on a table, then sashayed upstairs.
They whirled through the attic like three spinning tops
Partnered by a broom, a feather duster, a mop.
They called for a twmpath, clog-danced on the roof,
Shimmied with the staff-owl – all strutting their stuff.
They belly-danced, swooped into salsa and tango,
Clattered back downstairs in a noisy fandango.
They soft-shoed a shuffle over each of the chairs,
High-kicked and cartwheeled, alone and in pairs.
They hokeyed and cokeyed and jumped in and out,
Bent knees, stretched limbs, shook their bodies about.
They stomped and they stamped and bounced off the wall,
Then pranced a fierce polka out into the hall.

They swirled and they skirled, yet still wanted more,
So they turned a mazurka, hornpiped out the door.
They be-bopped, they jived, they jigged a fast jig,
Morris-danced on the grass with a troupe of Coydwig.
Then fair folk and elven, water and wood-sprite
Came silken-shoed, slip-sliding into the night.
They leapt over toadstools, limboed the brambles,
Maypoled through avenues of bright glow-worm candles.
The trees tossed their branches and sang out a tune
To the twinkle-toed stars, the mirror-ball moon.
Even the Gobbling were caught in the spell –
They sword-danced and clod-hopped – but not very well.
Witch Hakin stepped forward and danced up a storm
Of strobe-lightning, rain-beat, wind loud as a horn.

She brandished her staff-owl, choreographed creation
Through a dervish of dancing in strictest formation.
Said Mr Barafundle: *My feet are like bricks.*
The staff-owl claimed dizziness made him feel sick.
Young Stackpole was flagging and stifled a yawn,
As Hakin rubbed her bunions, called: *Time to go home!*
At the edge of the forest, all of the trees
Picked up their skirts, their petticoats of leaves,
They rustled them high, they rustled them low,
They rustled them fast, they rustled them slow.
They tore up the ground, ripped themselves free,
Lashed out with their roots, flashed knobbly knees.
As they all waved goodbye, the whole forest sang:
Never say can't-can't when you could say can-can.

Mr Barafundle and Stackpole panted breathlessly, as silence, shadow, stillness settled once more over the forest behind them. The rotating moon became steadfast, stars a static sparkle.

'It was wonderful.'

Stackpole folded back his weary wings, flexed his throbbing spine, wiggled his tired toes and stretched his aching tail until the scales rippled like a crimson stream.

'Yes . . . and now you've tried . . . you'll always be able . . . to dance,' puffed Mr Barafundle. 'Look . . . that magic potion rubbed off your talons hours ago.'

Stackpole gazed down. It was true. He tripped into a few steps, slowly, lightly.

'You see. Fantastic!' said Mr Barafundle. 'The champion rock-dancing-dragon of the world.'

Slowly, lightly, Stackpole and Mr Barafundle danced a last minuet together.

To and fro, to and fro
      along highways and byways,
beneath castles, through caves,
      over rivers, around hamlets,
down valleys, up hills,
      across meadows, past bays,
all night and all day
      until, at last, they reached
the headland where they met.

Stackpole's dancing faltered. He sniffed, he hiccupped, he gave a so-sad-sob. A tear plopped from the end of his snout onto one of Mr Barafundle's big, brown boots.

'Now, now,' said Mr Barafundle.

He touched Stackpole's shoulder oh-so-gently.

'I have a hammock on my island . . . just right for a worn-out rockdragon to rest in while he waits for the dragon-flock's return.'

Stackpole's eyes grew round and shiny.

'I c-couldn't possibly put you to all that t-trouble,' he stuttered hopefully.

'Of course you can,' said Mr Barafundle.